EAST
TO THE
SEA

Written and Illustrated by
Heidi Jardine Stoddart

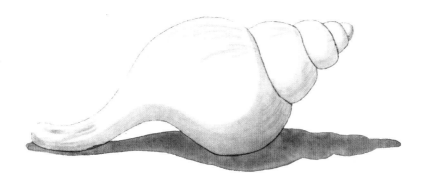

Dedicated to...
Mom, Dad, Tracy & Sherri for those cherished summers in St.Martins;
Megan, Jordan, Riley, Matthew & Hailey, my beachcombing buddies;
...And especially to Dwayne,
for believing & making dreams come true.

Library and Archives of Canada Cataloguing in Publication
Stoddart, Heidi, 1967-
East to the sea / Heidi Stoddart.
For children.
Casebound ISBN: 1-894372-42-5
Perfectbound ISBN: 1-894372-41-7
I. Title.
PS8637.T64E38 2004   jC813'.6   C2004-903326-3

DreamCatcher Publishing, Inc.
105 Prince William Street
Saint John, New Brunswick, Canada, E2L 2B2
www.dreamcatcherbooks.ca

Design by Lise Hansen
Printed and bound in Canada

With special thanks to Judi Pennanen for her teaching and encouragement,
& to Lise Hansen for magically bringing everything together.

EAST
TO THE
SEA

Written and Illustrated by
Heidi Jardine Stoddart

When I was young, about eight or nine,
My family went east in the summertime.
It was summer vacation for my sisters and me,
So my family packed up and drove east to the sea.

Three sisters in back, pajamas already on,
Mom and Dad took turns driving from dusk until dawn,
Through large glowing cities, by Great shimmering Lakes,
Past lonely farmhouses and grand seaway scapes.

A quick stop in the village at Grampie's old store,
Where Mom made us treat bags full of candy galore!
Next stop, "The Cottage", we knew from years past.

"Are we there yet?"
"How much further?"
"Please Daddy, drive fast!"

When at last - "There's the cottage!" - we'd arrived once again.

Our down east vacation could officially begin.

Weather-worn by sea winds and salt-water aged...

The cottage looked perfect because nothing had changed.

Days filled with sunshine were spent at the beach;

With cousins we'd search for shells safe from tide's reach...

Build castles and sail ships as seagulls would fly...

Climb mountains,

deep sea dive,

and soar through the sky.

Days damp with fog
meant a book by the fire,
Or games on the porch
as the tide came in higher,

Then trips in to town
to get more supplies,
Where local traditions
left us wide-eyed.

Warm nights -- to the beach, holding hands in a row
With blankets and jackets and flashlights in tow.
The dim night felt scary, dark shadows beside us,
But the sound of the waves and the lighthouse would guide us.

At last we arrived at the bonfire location,
Built in the daylight with great anticipation.
Dad struck a match, driftwood lit up the night,
Sparking and crackling with all of its might.

As we watched the sparks spiral and dance, heaven-bound,
My sister leaned over, with a whispering sound,
Said, "That's how the stars got to be in the sky.
They were bonfire sparks that went up too high."

We'd settle in cozy, as waves lapped nearby
And stars spread like gold dust across the night sky,
Singing and laughing as hotdogs were roasted...
Fingers fast sticky from marshmallows toasted.

As the flames ceased their leaping and embers grew bright,
We begged for the story Dad told us each night
About a huge sea monster out on the waves
Who spent moonlit hours digging holes called "The Caves".

"She's timid of people – stays away in the day.
When you go to bed, that's when she likes to play.
She frolics. She splashes. She digs holes 'round here too.
But a wee hole to her is a cave next to you!"

Eyes wide with wonder we'd near burst with fright.

Would Sea Monster come... to this beach... on this night?

"Time to pack up," Dad would say with a grin.

"Quick. To the cottage. Did I see a fin?"

Tucked under covers in the cot, my Mom said,
"It was another big day. It's past time for bed."
But not for the grown-ups. I'd drowsily try
To stay up and listen as stories would fly.

I'd catch bits of lore about old times and friends dear,
But eyes heavy with sleep, the tale's end I'd not hear,
For comforting voices, hushed laughter and waves
Soon lulled me to sleep after fresh salt air days.

Before we knew it, too quickly, the end would draw near.

A last walk by the ocean, I'd sigh, "See you next year."

Our seaside treasures, rocks smooth and shells white,
Soon filled our suitcases, packed safe and tight.

Just as good-byes were about to be heard,

We looked 'round for Grampie, who'd not said a word.

"He went for the mail," Nanny shared-with a kiss.

"Good-byes are too hard, something he'd rather miss."

The trip home seemed much longer, our Mom always said.

No longer excitement, there was quiet instead,

For we were remembering days happily spent

At the seaside, so thoughts took us back, not ahead.

I've now grown much older,
but still to this day,
I cherish those times
spent on that ocean Bay,
Content such adventures
once again will be known,
For our next generation
is creating their own.